GEORGE
the Hero Hound

By Jeffrey Ebbeler

two lions

To my sister, Julie, and her pony,
the original Rusty Dusty Rover Red George

Published by Two Lions, New York

www.apub.com

Amazon, the Amazon logo, and Two Lions are trademarks of Amazon.com, Inc.,
or its affiliates.

ISBN-13: 9781503941762
ISBN-10: 1503941760

The illustrations are rendered in acrylics, ink, and pencil
on Fabriano hot press watercolor paper.

Book design by Jen Keenan
Printed in China

First Edition

10 9 8 7 6 5 4 3 2 1

George was a good old hound dog.

Every day George was up, even before the chickens,
to help old Farmer Fritz with the chores. That rust-bucket
tractor was always falling apart . . .

and those wily cows were always plotting
to get out and feast on the cornfield.

But George didn't mind a whit, as long as he got his afternoon nap. He had a good life for a hound dog.

Until the day old Farmer Fritz decided to retire and move to a cabana on the beach where they didn't allow cows, they didn't allow pigs, and, sad to say, they didn't even allow dogs.

George was left in the dust.

But not for long. Nothing could have prepared George for the Gladstone family. They'd packed up their noisy apartment in the city and bought Fritz Farm: cows, pigs, George, and all.

George could tell right away that the Gladstone family would need a whole heap of help. There'd be no afternoon naps on the porch for a while.

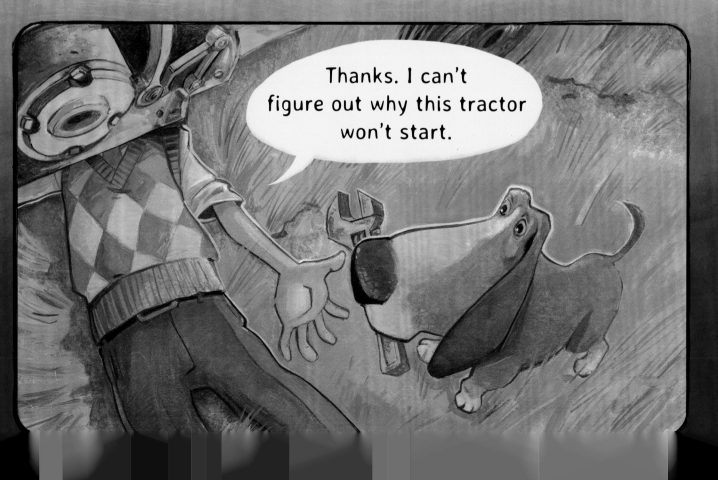

Crash!

George watched as the tractor went clean through the fence. But he wouldn't let the cows get away on his watch!

He spent the next couple hours
trying to herd those sneaky cows
back into their pen, where they belonged.

George was tuckered out. All he wanted was a cool drink of water and to sneak a few winks in the shade.

George was swept out of the house in a cloud of dust.

George shook himself off and was just padding toward his favorite shady spot when he spied something blue.

Then Owen came running over.

I was supposed to be watching my baby sister, Olive. Can you help me find her, boy?

George took a good sniff of Olive's ribbon—he was a hound dog, after all—and off they went.

After searching **high** and **low**…

they finally found that pint-size rambler.

George had saved the day! As he trotted back home, George was sure he would finally, definitely get his well-deserved nap.

Until...

Crash!

From that day on,
George still didn't get
many afternoon naps.

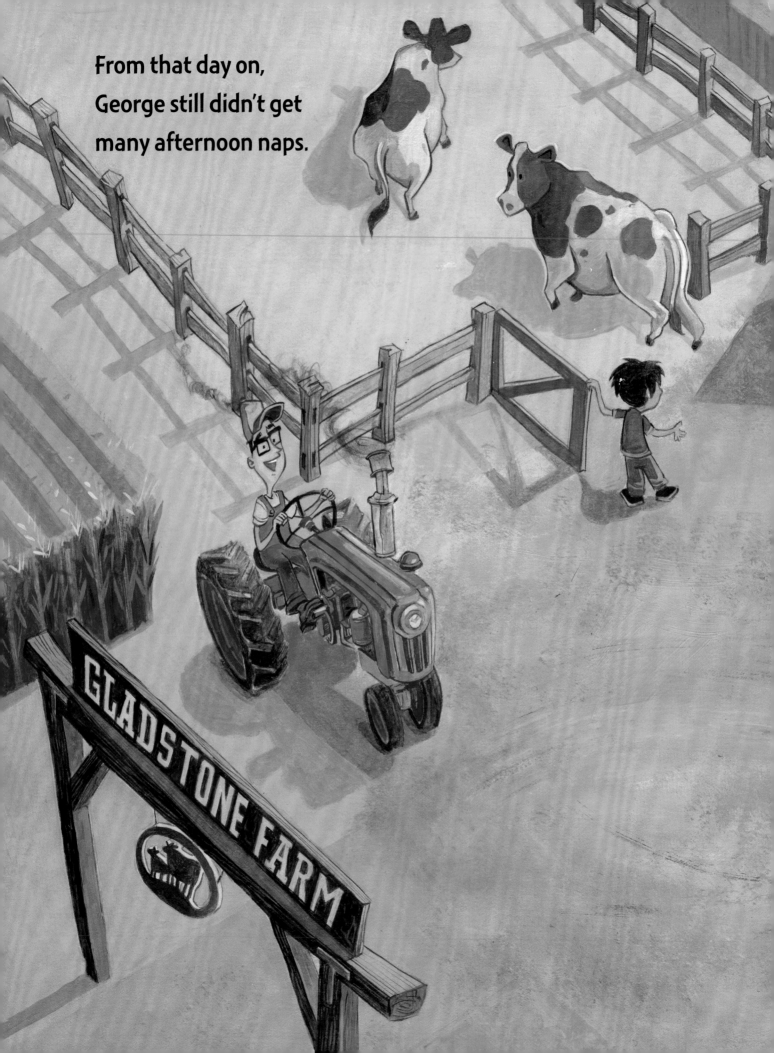

But he didn't mind too much.
Turns out that he liked herding Olive
a lot more than he liked herding cows.

And since George figured the Gladstones needed some tips on how to run the farm, he vowed to teach them everything he knew.

Especially how to deal with those crafty cows.

his name!